MARK GRACE
FIRST BASEMAN
ARIZONA DIAMONDBACKS

RANDY JOHNSON
PITCHER
ARIZONA DIAMONDBACKS

THE STORY OF THE ARIZONA DIAMONDBACKS

Published by Creative Education
P.O. Box 227, Mankato, Minnesota 56002
Creative Education is an imprint of The Creative Company
www.thecreativecompany.us

Design and production by Blue Design
Art direction by Rita Marshall
Printed by Corporate Graphics in the United States of America

Photographs by Getty Images (Brian Bahr, Al Bello/Allsport, Jonathan Daniel/Allsport, Stephen Dunn, Elsa, Mike Fiala/AFP, Stephen Green/MLB Photos, Jeff Gross/Allsport, Harry How/Allsport, Jed Jacobsohn, Jed Jacobsohn/Allsport, Vincent Laforet/Allsport, Rob Leiter/MLB Photos, John G. Mabanglo/AFP, David Maxwell/AFP, Donald Miralle, Christian Petersen, Tom Pidgeon, Ezra Shaw, Don Smith/MLB Photos, Paul Spinelli/MLB Photos, Dilip Vishwanat)

Library of Congress Cataloging-in-Publication Data

Gilbert, Sara.
The story of the Arizona Diamondbacks / by Sara Gilbert.
p. cm. — (Baseball: the great American game)
Includes index.
Summary: The history of the Arizona Diamondbacks professional baseball team from its inaugural 1998 season to today, spotlighting the team's greatest players and most memorable moments.
ISBN 978-1-60818-031-8
1. Arizona Diamondbacks (Baseball team)—History—Juvenile literature. I. Title. II. Series.

GV875.A64G55 2011
796.357'640979173—dc22   2010023560

CPSIA: 110310 PO1381

First Edition
2 4 6 8 9 7 5 3 1

Page 3: Pitcher Curt Schilling
Page 4: Shortstop Stephen Drew

BASEBALL: THE GREAT AMERICAN GAME

THE STORY OF THE ARIZONA DIAMONDBACKS

Sara Gilbert

CREATIVE EDUCATION

CONTENTS

A HOT START

The heat is almost always on in Phoenix, Arizona. Temperatures in the desert city soar to 100 °F or higher on an average of 90 days each year, sometimes reaching up to 120 °F or even more scorching. So arid is the city that the Navajo American Indians called it *Hoozdo*, which translates to "the place is hot." During the winter months, that heat is appreciated by the many people who travel south to escape the cold and snow of more northerly states. The dozen Major League Baseball teams that start their spring training camps in the state of Arizona in February each year also appreciate it.

Until 1998, the end of spring training meant the end of the big-league baseball season for Arizona fans. But on March 31 of that year, Phoenix celebrated the start of a new season with a major-league team of its own: the Arizona Diamondbacks, named after the region's native rattlesnakes. The newest addition to the National League (NL) had been almost four years in the making, as baseball had decided to expand by two franchises in 1994.

Bank One Ballpark, later renamed Chase Field, made sports history as the first stadium in America to feature a retractable roof.

PITCHER · RANDY JOHNSON

With his wild hair, shaggy moustache, and towering height, Randy Johnson was intimidating even before he started pitching. But when "The Big Unit" unleashed his 100-mile-per-hour fastball, he could flat-out terrorize opposing batters. That's exactly what he did during the eight seasons that he spent with the Diamondbacks. On May 8, 2001, Johnson fanned 20 batters in 1 game, and he led the majors in strikeouts with 372 that season. During each of his first four seasons with Arizona, his numerous accomplishments on the mound were honored with the NL Cy Young Award. He left Arizona in 2004 but returned before the 2007 season.

RANDY JOHNSON
PITCHER

ARIZONA DIAMONDBACKS

STATS

Diamondbacks seasons: 1999–2004, 2007–08

Height: 6-foot-10

Weight: 225

- 5-time Cy Young Award winner

- 10-time All-Star

- Pitched a perfect game (May 18, 2004)

- 303–166 career record

The Diamondbacks lineup that took the field on opening day 1998 had been carefully assembled by wealthy team owner Jerry Colangelo, who wanted the club to be competitive immediately. He gave lucrative contracts to second baseman Jay Bell and third baseman Matt Williams, but it was the other corner of the infield—first base—that really demonstrated Colangelo's commitment to winning. The owner offered unsigned rookie Travis Lee a $10-million contract that raised eyebrows around the league.

Lee proved his worth during Arizona's first game at the brand new, $354-million Bank One Ballpark, commonly called "the BOB." He posted the team's first hit, first home run, and first run batted in (RBI). However, the game ended 9–2 in favor of the Colorado Rockies. Four losses later, the Diamondbacks finally recorded their first franchise win—a 3–2 victory for Andy Benes, a veteran hurler who led the pitching staff with 14 wins that first season. The team finished 65–97, landing in fifth place in the NL Western Division.

Colangelo and general manager Joe Garagiola made a concerted effort to improve the Diamondbacks' fortunes in the off-season. By the time spring training started in 1999, they had inked deals with several

top-notch players—most notably veteran pitchers Randy Johnson and Todd Stottlemyre and center fielder Steve Finley, who was already a multiple Gold Glove winner. Colangelo and Garagiola had also orchestrated trades that brought in steady-hitting left fielder Luis Gonzalez and speedy shortstop Tony Womack.

These additions brought much-needed experience to the team. Even returning veterans such as Bell and Williams played better in their company. Bell led the team with 38 home runs in 1999, closely followed by Williams's 35 dingers. Finley, never before known as a power hitter, added 34 of his own, and Gonzalez impressed his new fans with a breakout season: a .336 average, 26 home runs, a league-leading 206 hits, and 111 RBI. "We were hoping for maybe .270 to .280, 15 homers, and 70 RBI," Colangelo said of "Gonzo." "Needless to say, we're pretty happy with the way things have worked out."

As potent as the offense was, however, it was the pitching staff that had improved the most. Johnson tallied 17 wins, led the majors with 364 strikeouts, and led the league with a 2.48 earned run average (ERA)— numbers that made him the easy choice for the NL Cy Young Award as the league's best pitcher.

LUIS GONZALEZ

"Gonzo" became an Arizona fan favorite as he slugged his way toward career totals of 354 homers and 596 doubles. In 2010, the Diamondbacks announced that he would be the first Arizona player to have his jersey number (20) retired.

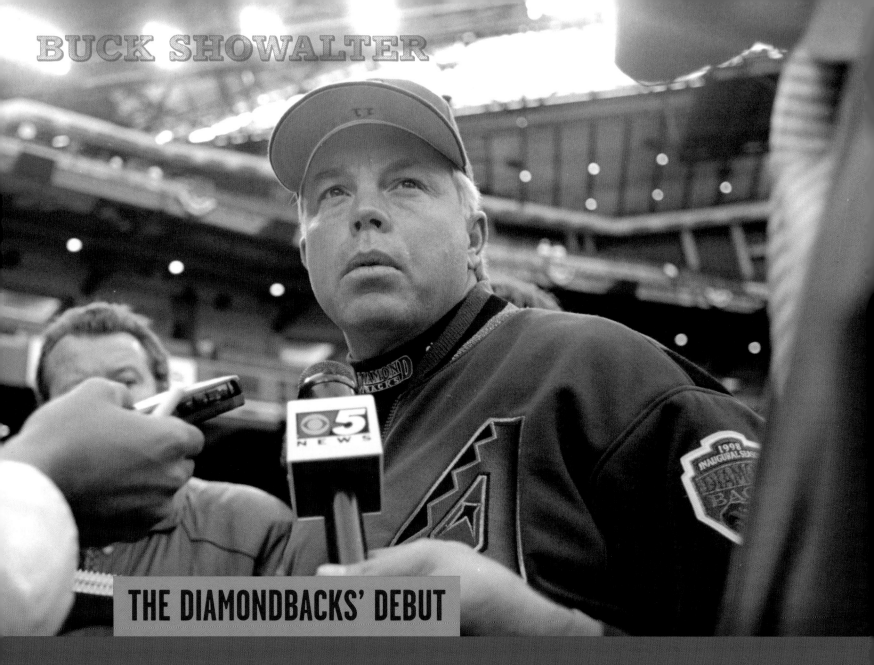

THE DIAMONDBACKS' DEBUT

The Arizona Diamondbacks had been in the making for the better part of three years before the team finally took the field on March 31, 1998. Although it lost that first game and the next four as well, the team played valiantly in its first major-league season. The Diamondbacks made headlines in a May game when manager Buck Showalter, clinging to an 8–6 lead, decided to intentionally walk fearsome San Francisco Giants slugger Barry Bonds with the bases loaded in the bottom of the ninth inning, even though it meant cutting the lead to one by sending a run home. Showalter's move paid off, as the next batter lined out to right field to end the game. Such savvy strategy helped the team look less like an expansion club and more like a rising contender. In September, Arizona recorded wins in 12 of the 24 games it played, including 7 in a row. Although the Diamondbacks finished the season in last place in the NL West at 65–97, the groundwork for a winning team had been laid—and the fans were happy. The Diamondbacks played 21 home games in front of a sold-out stadium and drew more than 3.6 million fans in their first season.

CATCHER · DAMIAN MILLER

It takes a special kind of catcher to handle the blistering fastballs hurled by Randy Johnson. But Damian Miller was up to the task. Miller, who played his first major-league season with the Minnesota Twins in 1997 before going to Arizona in baseball's 1998 expansion draft, became known as Johnson's personal backstop because of the skillful manner in which he handled the 6-foot-10, flamethrowing pitcher. But excellent glove work was not Miller's only strength; he could also hold his own at the plate. He maintained a .270 or better batting average in four of his five years in a Diamondbacks uniform.

DAMIAN MILLER
CATCHER

ARIZONA
DIAMONDBACKS

STATS

Diamondbacks seasons: 1998–2002

Height: 6-foot-3

Weight: 202

- **2002 All-Star**

- **406 career RBI**

- **.262 career BA**

- **205 career doubles**

FIRST BASEMAN · MARK GRACE

Mark Grace joined the Diamondbacks at just the right time. After 13 years with the Chicago Cubs, the joke-cracking, Gold Glove-winning, steady-hitting first baseman needed a change of scenery and signed with Arizona following the 2000 season. In his first year with the team, "Amazing Grace" hit .298 with 78 RBI and helped the Diamondbacks win a world championship—the first of his career. Grace, always respected for his consistency rather than his flashiness, ended his 16-year career after the 2003 season with a lifetime on-base percentage of .383, almost 2,500 hits, and more than 500 doubles.

MARK GRACE
FIRST BASEMAN

ARIZONA
DIAMONDBACKS

STATS

Diamondbacks seasons: 2001–03

Height: 6-foot-2

Weight: 190

- 3-time All-Star

- 4-time Gold Glove winner

- .303 career BA

- 2,445 career hits

With so many players enjoying career-best seasons, the Diamondbacks secured the division lead early. Gonzalez put together a 30-game hitting streak that lasted from April 11 until May 20, helping the team finish the month of May with 18 wins and first-place status in the NL West. By season's end, the Diamondbacks were 100–62 and had achieved the fastest ascent (two seasons) to a division championship in major-league history.

In the playoffs, Arizona met the New York Mets in a best-of-five NL Division Series (NLDS). The teams split the first two games in Arizona before heading to "The Big Apple" for Games 3 and 4. But there the Diamondbacks' luck ran out. The Mets won the next two games, including one in which an extra-inning home run slipped out of Finley's usually flawless glove and cost Arizona the game.

Diamondbacks manager Buck Showalter tried to reassure his players that better days were ahead, but he couldn't have foreseen the injuries that would slow the team in 2000. Williams, Stottlemyre, and closer Matt Mantei were each sidelined for significant stretches of time. Johnson, who put together another Cy Young Award-winning season, got some help when the team acquired star pitcher Curt Schilling in July, yet Arizona finished third in the NL West. Showalter was fired soon after, and Colangelo started looking for a new leader.

CLIMBING TO THE TOP

ew Arizona manager Bob Brenly, a former big-league catcher, coach, and radio and television broadcaster, opened his spring training meeting in 2001 by presenting a pair of new rules, which he had scrawled on a cocktail napkin, to his players: "Be on time" and "Get it done."

Veteran players, including newly acquired first baseman Mark Grace and right fielder Reggie Sanders, responded especially well to Brenly's more relaxed approach. Gonzo enjoyed a monster season, sending 57 balls into the stands and driving in 142 runs. Johnson and Schilling combined for 43 wins, accounting for almost half of the team's total victories, and South Korean closer Byung-Hyun Kim notched 19 saves. During the final week of the season, the Diamondbacks clinched their second division championship and charged into the NLDS against the St. Louis Cardinals.

Schilling pitched a three-hit complete game as Arizona won the first contest 1–0, but the Cardinals came back to win 4–1 in Game 2. Second baseman Craig Counsell's three-run homer in Game 3 gave the Diamondbacks another win, but St. Louis won the next contest to force

BOB BRENLY

As Arizona's skipper, Brenly could relate to players at all positions. Not only did he have a personable managerial style, but as a big-league player in the 1980s, he had spent time at catcher, first base, third base, and all outfield positions.

SECOND BASEMAN · CRAIG COUNSELL

Although it had been only three years since he scored the winning run of the 1997 World Series for the Florida Marlins, Craig Counsell was in a slump when he joined the Diamondbacks in 2000. To get out of it, he developed an unusual batting stance: he stood with his six-foot frame barely bent, lifted his arms shoulder high, pointed his bat straight up, and then wagged it back and forth. Thanks to that stance, "the Pancake" (his well-worn, floppy glove), and his stints with five different teams, Counsell became one of the most recognizable players in baseball.

STATS

Diamondbacks seasons: 2000–03, 2005–06

Height: 6 feet

Weight: 180

- **.985 career fielding percentage**

- **2001 NLCS MVP**

- **.257 career BA**

- **381 career RBI**

CRAIG COUNSELL
SECOND BASEMAN

ARIZONA
DIAMONDBACKS

a deciding fifth game. Game 5 was played at the BOB, where Arizona won 2–1. "We gave the fans everything they could want in this series," said Schilling, who pitched all nine innings of the final game.

If Schilling was the star of the NLDS, Johnson was the hero of the 2001 NL Championship Series (NLCS) against the Atlanta Braves. As Schilling had done in the previous series, Johnson pitched a three-hit complete game in Game 1, setting the stage for a four-games-to-one series victory that sent the Diamondbacks to the World Series to face the heavily favored New York Yankees.

The first two games were played in Phoenix, where Schilling and Johnson combined for a one-two knockout of the Yankees. In Game 1, Schilling yielded only three hits in seven innings, and Gonzo's two-run homer powered the Diamondbacks to a 9–1 win. The next night, Johnson struck out 11 batters in a decisive 4–0 victory. With a two-game lead, Arizona went east to play in the venerable but raucous Yankee Stadium. "We know they're not going to open their arms and welcome us in a friendly way," Gonzalez said. "I think there will be no bigger thrill than walking out to Yankee Stadium and knowing that the crowd hates us."

The city of New York was still reeling from the terror attacks of September 11, 2001, when the Diamondbacks arrived in town at the end of October. The team paid its respects at Ground Zero before the series started and then watched president George W. Bush throw out the ceremonial first pitch before Game 3, which Arizona lost 2–1. Schilling tried to make up for that in Game 4. He held the Yankees to one run through seven innings, but Kim gave up a two-run home run that tied the score and forced extra innings. Yankees shortstop Derek Jeter ended the game with a shot into the right-field stands in the 10th. Game 5 also went extra frames before the Yanks pulled out a 3–2 win. With New York up three games to two, the series headed back to Arizona.

In Game 6, the Diamondbacks scored 15 runs on 22 hits, while Johnson held the Yankees to just 2 runs. Game 7 pitted Schilling against Yankees ace Roger Clemens. The future Hall-of-Famers kept the game scoreless until the sixth inning, when Arizona outfielder Danny Bautista doubled in a run. After the Yanks scored twice, Miguel Batista took over for Schilling. Batista got just 1 man out before an unexpected

THIRD BASEMAN · MATT WILLIAMS

In 1986, the San Francisco Giants selected Matt Williams with the third overall pick of the amateur draft. Twelve years later, when he joined the Diamondbacks in 1998, he was known for his ability to drive home runs to all parts of the field. But long balls weren't his only specialty; Williams was also a slick fielder who manned the hot corner of the infield so well that he earned four Gold Gloves. Although injuries and an arthritis-like condition slowed his production toward the end of his career, he was nonetheless an important part of Arizona's 2001 world championship team.

MATT WILLIAMS
THIRD BASEMAN

ARIZONA
DIAMONDBACKS

STATS

Diamondbacks seasons: 1998–2003

Height: 6-foot-2

Weight: 210

- **5-time All-Star**
- **4-time Gold Glove winner**
- **378 career HR**
- **1,218 career RBI**

FOUR-YEAR FORMULA

After failing to lead Arizona to the top in the franchise's first three seasons, manager Buck Showalter was replaced in 2001 by Bob Brenly, who had no experience as a major-league skipper. If that seems a bit unorthodox, consider the team he was managing. Not a single regular player had been developed in Arizona's minor league affiliates, which groom prospects for the big leagues. Instead, the four-year-old team was populated by seasoned veterans, such as second baseman Jay Bell and third baseman Matt Williams, who had been lured with large salaries and the promise of playing for

a competitive team. It soon became apparent that they were: in 2001, Arizona clinched the NL West crown for a second time, and by the end of October, the Diamondbacks were on their way to the World Series after defeating the St. Louis Cardinals in the NLDS and overtaking the Atlanta Braves in the NLCS. And by November 4, the Diamondbacks were celebrating a seven-game World Series victory over the New York Yankees. "We did everything we could to get the job done," said team owner Jerry Colangelo. "The opportunity was there, so we went for it."

The Diamondbacks' 2001 title was cause for big celebration in Arizona, as it was the first major pro sports championship in the state's history.

reliever was called in: Randy Johnson, who was less than 24 hours removed from his last pitching performance. Despite having a weary arm, Johnson retired all four batters he faced. But in the bottom of the ninth, New York still held a 2–1 lead with the team's ace closer, Mariano Rivera, on the mound.

Mark Grace led off the inning with a single. Then catcher Damian Miller reached first on a fielder's choice. One out later, Womack doubled, which allowed Miller to score and tie the game. When Gonzalez stepped to the plate, all Arizona needed was a base hit. And Gonzo obliged, sending a bloop single into shallow center to drive home the winning run. Only four years into their existence, the Diamondbacks had won a world championship. "From day one, our goal wasn't just to get to the World Series," Gonzalez said after the game. "It was to win it." Three days later, a parade in Copper Square drew more than 300,000 exuberant fans, all eager to congratulate their heroes of summer.

REBUILDING MODE

rizona's fans were expecting the same sort of success the following season. Most of the team's key players returned, and management bolstered the pitching staff by signing right-handed starter Rick Helling and relief specialist Mike Myers during the off-season. But before spring training was over, Williams and Bell had suffered leg injuries, and reserve first baseman Erubiel Durazo had broken his wrist. In May, a shoulder injury knocked Bautista out of the lineup for the remainder of the season.

Despite such setbacks, the 2002 Diamondbacks took the top spot in the division in May and hovered there for most of the summer, thanks to the fine pitching of Johnson and Schilling. But more injuries—Counsell missing the last two months of the season with a pinched nerve that required surgery and Gonzalez separating his shoulder while making a sliding catch—slowed Arizona's pace to the title. It took until the second-to-last game of the season for the weakened Diamondbacks to secure the division crown.

Outfielder David Dellucci wore a Diamondbacks uniform from 1998 to 2003. As a hitter, he had a knack for finding outfield gaps, and in his first season in the desert, he ripped a league-leading 12 triples for the expansion Arizona team.

SHORTSTOP · TONY WOMACK

Tony Womack was every catcher's nightmare. Arizona's compact, fleet-footed shortstop made stealing bases into an art form. He had to learn to play in the outfield when he first joined the team in 1999, since the middle infield was already well staffed. But his productivity on the bases was more important to the team than anything else. In his first season with the Diamondbacks, he led the league with a career-high 72 stolen bases. That same season, he used his quick feet to notch an inside-the-park grand slam that turned a 4–3 Arizona deficit into an unlikely 7–4 victory against the Houston Astros.

STATS

Diamondbacks seasons: 1999–2003

Height: 5-foot-9

Weight: 160

- **3-time NL leader in steals**
- **363 career stolen bases**
- **1997 All-Star**
- **24-game hitting streak in 2001**

TONY WOMACK
SHORTSTOP

ARIZONA
DIAMONDBACKS

By then, the team was so battered that it was no match for the Cardinals in the NLDS. St. Louis made quick work of the Diamondbacks, sweeping the series in three games. Things didn't improve before the 2003 season, either. Early in the spring, Johnson was placed on the disabled list with an inflamed right knee. Then Schilling had to have an emergency surgery and, a month later, broke a bone in his pitching hand. Four other position players, including Counsell, also spent time on the disabled list in June.

Suddenly, the formerly veteran-heavy team was populated with youngsters called up from the minor leagues. Thirteen rookies debuted during the 2003 season, including pitcher Brandon Webb, who won 10 games and posted a 2.84 ERA. Despite Webb's valiant efforts and the midseason acquisitions of first baseman Shea Hillenbrand and outfielder Raul Mondesi, Arizona couldn't climb back into contention. The season ended respectably, 84–78, but Arizona was left out of the playoff picture.

Arizona management set about revamping the roster in the off-season, this time looking for power and youth. Schilling was sent to

LEFT FIELDER · LUIS GONZALEZ

Before he was traded to the Diamondbacks in 1999, Luis Gonzalez was a solid contact hitter better known for line drives than home runs. But when "Gonzo" came to Arizona, the skinny outfielder turned into a home-run-hitting slugger. In 2001, he helped catapult the Diamondbacks to the World Series with 57 home runs, 142 RBI, and a .325 batting average. Despite that power, it took only a bloop single off Gonzalez's bat to drive in the dramatic, series-clinching run in Game 7, making the Diamondbacks world champions in just their fourth year of existence.

LUIS GONZALEZ
LEFT FIELDER

ARIZONA
DIAMONDBACKS

STATS

Diamondbacks seasons: 1999–2006

Height: 6-foot-2

Weight: 180

- 5-time All-Star

- 30-game hitting streak in 1999

- 1999 NL hits leader (206)

- 2001 Silver Slugger award winner

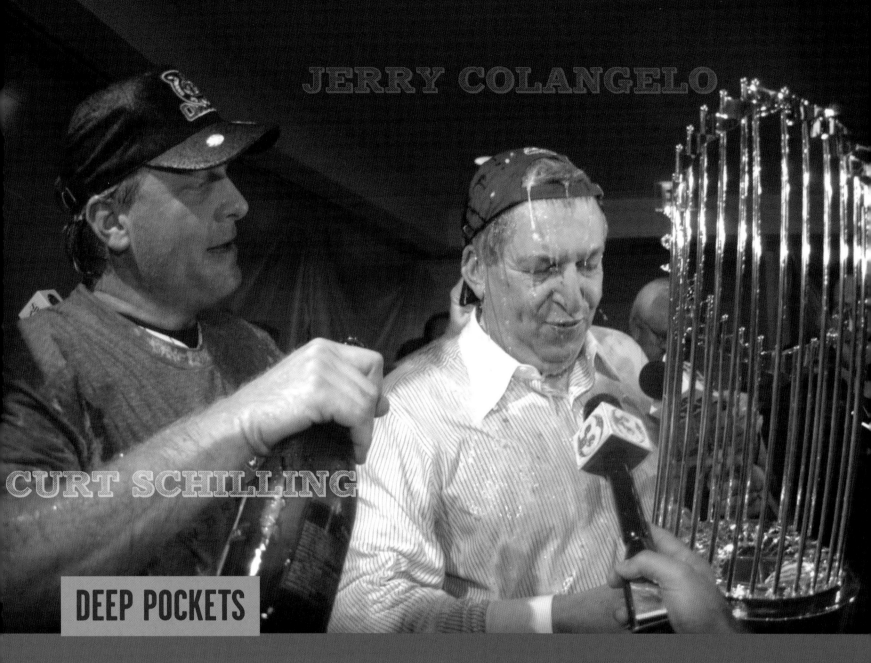

CURT SCHILLING

DEEP POCKETS

It took more than raw talent to turn the Diamondbacks into world champions in just four years. It also took a tremendous financial commitment from the team's owner, who paid dearly to produce a winning team in Arizona. Although many owners were appalled at the salaries Jerry Colangelo was willing to offer, he was determined to pay for perfection. Before the team's debut in 1998, he paid former Kansas City Royals shortstop Jay Bell $34 million to play at second base for 5 years and Cleveland Indians third baseman Matt Williams $49.5 million for 6 years—deals that Colangelo said had as much to do with their character as with their playing ability. He dug even deeper in 1999, when he negotiated a 4-year, $52-million contract with star pitcher Randy Johnson, making him the second-highest-paid player in baseball at the time, and offered outfielder Steve Finley a 5-year, $25.5-million contract. By the time the 1999 season started, the team's payroll was at $65.9 million—more than twice what it had been in 1998. Although continuing drop-offs in season ticket sales left the team hurting for money, Colangelo's plan eventually worked. The Diamondbacks won the NL West in 1999, and by 2001, on an $81-million budget, they became World Series champions.

DIAMONDBACKS

[29]

Scott Hairston added youthful energy to the Diamondbacks' 2004 lineup, starting 83 games at second base as just a rookie.

SCOTT HAIRSTON

the Boston Red Sox for two young pitchers, and six players were traded to the Milwaukee Brewers in exchange for slugging first baseman Richie Sexson. "It's going to be exciting," Arizona general manager Joe Garagiola said of the acquisitions. "This will give our whole lineup a very different look."

The 2004 Arizona lineup did indeed feature several new faces, with Sexson at first, Scott Hairston at second, Chad Tracy at third, veteran Roberto Alomar playing a utility role, and Luis Terrero with Gonzo and Finley in the outfield. But the cornerstone of that makeover didn't last long. Just days after hitting the longest home run (503 feet) in Chase Field (as the BOB was renamed in 2005) history in April, Sexson partially dislocated his shoulder during a check swing. When he attempted to make a comeback in May, he re-aggravated the injury and had to have surgery, effectively ending his season.

Amid all the changes around the field, Johnson remained the main man on the mound. Unfortunately, the rotation behind him no longer had much depth. Webb posted only 7 wins, second-best to Johnson's 16, and no other pitcher managed even 5 victories. After enduring a 14-

THE PERFECT GAME

As 40-year-old Randy Johnson took the mound at Atlanta's Turner Field on the night of May 18, 2004, his biggest goal was to record a win. After four consecutive Cy Young Award-winning seasons with the Diamondbacks, Johnson had suffered through a miserable, injury-plagued season in 2003 and had been subject to criticism over his 3–4 start in 2004. But on that spring night against the Atlanta Braves, Johnson silenced his critics the best way possible: by eliminating all 27 batters he faced and throwing the 17th perfect game in major-league history—the first no-hitter of any sort for the Arizona franchise. The Big Unit struck out 13 batters and threw 18 pitches that were clocked at 97 miles per hour or faster—including a 98-mile-per-hour fastball that pinch hitter Eddie Perez swung through for the last out of the game. He ended the game having tossed a total of 117 pitches, more than half of them for strikes. Johnson, who had pitched a no-hitter 14 years earlier as an up-and-coming member of the Seattle Mariners, seemed unfazed by the achievement as his teammates crowded around him with congratulations. "Not bad for being 40 years old," he said.

RANDY JOHNSON

game midseason losing streak, the Diamondbacks finished 2004 with a dismal 51–111 mark, at the bottom of the heap in the NL West.

In an effort to climb back to the top, the Diamondbacks made two major moves before the 2005 season, hiring former Arizona bench coach Bob Melvin as manager and trading Johnson to the Yankees. Arizona also signed slugging third baseman Troy Glaus, who hit 37 home runs for his new team in 2005. Glaus and infielder Tony Clark helped Arizona make a 26-game improvement over the previous season. But even though the Diamondbacks' record of 77–85 demonstrated a move in the right direction, the team remained out of the playoffs.

Webb, who had doubled his 2004 win total to 14 in 2005, became the team's undisputed star in 2006. The young pitcher led the league with 16 victories, received his first invitation to the All-Star Game, and took home the coveted Cy Young Award, providing a bright spot in an otherwise mediocre 76–86 season for Arizona. Webb's emergence as the staff ace helped blunt the loss of fan favorites Gonzalez and Counsell, who both played their final games in Arizona uniforms in 2006 before moving on to new teams.

CENTER FIELDER · STEVE FINLEY

Steve Finley was no stranger to grass stains. His speed and instincts helped him successfully track down and dive for balls that would have fallen in front of most other outfielders. Although such acrobatic fielding earned him five Gold Glove awards, it also caused him great pain. Finley suffered many nagging injuries but managed to play through most of them; in 1999, he hit two home runs in one game while suffering from a bulging disc in his back. The consistent line-drive hitter polished his home run stroke in Arizona: he homered 34 times in 1999 and 35 times in 2000.

STEVE FINLEY
CENTER FIELDER

ARIZONA
DIAMONDBACKS

STATS

Diamondbacks seasons: 1999–2004

Height: 6-foot-2

Weight: 180

- 2-time All-Star

- 5-time Gold Glove winner

- .988 career fielding percentage

- 304 career HR

COMEBACK KIDS

Webb's dominance was one of the reasons experts started predicting a turnaround for the Diamondbacks— although few thought it would happen quite as quickly as it did, considering that so many of the heroes who had helped the team claim early glory were now gone. Arizona returned to the field in 2007 sporting redesigned red-and-sand-colored uniforms, a combination that suited returning pitcher Randy Johnson well. Johnson—in the twilight of his career—had asked the Yankees to trade him back to Arizona so that he could be closer to his family in the area (he had lost his brother to a brain aneurysm during his tenure in New York), and his request was granted almost two years to the day after the original trade that had sent him to the East Coast.

Although Johnson and his wicked fastball were warmly

BRANDON WEBB

ORLANDO HUDSON

welcomed back to Phoenix, he struggled with back injuries that eventually required season-ending surgery in July. At the time, Johnson was among the NL's top 10 strikeout pitchers, but The Big Unit was soon overshadowed by Webb, who had another All-Star season with 18 wins and a 3.01 ERA. The Diamondbacks also received inspired play from second baseman Orlando Hudson and rookie center fielder Chris Young, who hit 32 home runs and stole 27 bases in his first full big-league season.

BASEBALL AT THE BOB

When Jerry Colangelo first met with baseball owners in 1993 to discuss bringing a major-league team to Arizona, he painted an idyllic picture of the park in which his team would play: a state-of-the-art stadium with a retractable roof, natural grass, and a swimming pool and jacuzzi for a select number of spectators just beyond the center-field wall. By the time ground was broken for the $354-million downtown Phoenix facility in November 1995, the plans had evolved even further. The field was designed with a dirt path between the pitcher's mound and home plate, reminiscent of early ballparks, and celebratory water cannons were added to the outfield. When the 49,033-seat stadium opened in March 1998, the roof moved in time with music composed to last exactly the four and a half minutes required to move the steel structure. The pool and spa, which got a facelift in 2005, have hosted more than 20,000 visitors—and a few long home runs as well. The first player to send a ball splashing into the pool was first baseman Mark Grace, who homered as a member of the Chicago Cubs on May 12, 1998. The stadium was renamed Chase Field in 2005.

RIGHT FIELDER · DANNY BAUTISTA

Danny Bautista had been bouncing around the major leagues for the better part of a decade when, in June 2000, he was traded to Arizona. A little stability did him good. He had the best offensive years of his career in the desert, hitting above .300 in 2000, 2001, and 2002. When the longtime reserve earned a starting spot in 2004, he showed his stuff by putting together a 21-game hitting streak and ended the season with a career-high 154 hits. Unfortunately, an ankle injury the following spring ended his career. Bautista officially retired in March 2005 at the age of 33.

STATS

Diamondbacks seasons: 2000–04

Height: 5-foot-11

Weight: 170

- **685 career hits**
- **319 career RBI**
- **.272 career BA**
- **.984 career fielding percentage**

DANNY BAUTISTA
RIGHT FIELDER

ARIZONA
DIAMONDBACKS

MANAGER · BOB BRENLY

Bob Brenly, a former catcher for the San Francisco Giants, started his first season as manager of the Diamondbacks with a team full of veteran players—some of whom were only 10 years his junior. Under his firmly controlled yet laid-back leadership, the 2001 Diamondbacks cruised to a 92–70 record, tops in the NL West, and upset the powerful New York Yankees in the World Series. Although Brenly's team repeated as division champs in 2002, he was fired after a midseason slide in 2004, and his managerial career came to an end.

STATS

Diamondbacks seasons as manager:
2001–04

Managerial record: 303–262

World Series championship: 2001

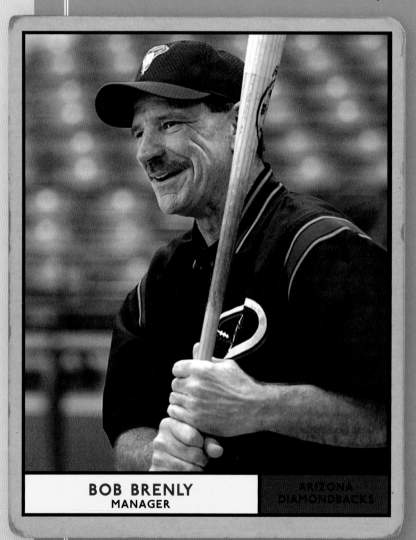

BOB BRENLY
MANAGER

ARIZONA
DIAMONDBACKS

The plucky young team won 50 games at home and another 40 on the road to post its best record since 2002 and capture the NL West title by a mere half game over the Rockies. But after sweeping the Chicago Cubs in the NLDS, the Diamondbacks found themselves facing the red-hot Rockies (who had won the Wild Card berth) in the NLCS. Colorado exacted revenge on its division rival by sweeping the series four games to none. As disappointed as the Diamondbacks were, they knew that they had exceeded expectations just by getting as far as they did. "It's something to write about," manager Bob Melvin told reporters after the NLCS. "Our offensive numbers weren't unbelievable as a whole. But there were two teams left in the National League, and we were one of them."

Arizona seemed headed for a second consecutive division title in 2008, especially after compiling an impressive 20–8 record by the end of April. Webb was again in fine form, winning his first 9 outings of the year and achieving a league-leading 22 wins for the season, and right-hander Dan Haren won a career-high 16 games in his first season with the Diamondbacks. Johnson recovered from his surgery to win 11 of the 30 games he started. But although the Diamondbacks had a slight lead in the NL West with a 47–48 record at the All-Star break, injuries to

Hudson and red-hot young outfielder Eric Byrnes proved costly in the long run. Arizona ended the season 82–80, just two games behind the Los Angeles Dodgers.

The young Diamondbacks entered the 2009 campaign as legitimate contenders for a division championship. The starting rotation, anchored by Webb and Haren, was expected by many to carry the team back to the top. Then Webb gave up six runs in just four innings on opening day because of pain in his pitching shoulder and ended up missing the rest of the season. To make matters worse, Byrnes' hand was broken when he was hit by a pitch in June, cutting his season short again. Haren led the team with 14 wins, and third baseman Mark Reynolds emerged as a powerhouse slugger, clubbing 44 home runs and posting 102 RBI. Yet just as quickly as it had returned to the top of the NL West standings, Arizona fell back to the bottom. The team's 70–92 record put it a full 25 games behind the dominant Dodgers.

But the Diamondbacks had no intention of staying mired in the basement. Webb continued working toward his return, and the bullpen was bolstered by the acquisition of right-hander Aaron Heilman. Although

COMING BACK FROM CANCER

During a routine physical on February 6, 2008, doctors felt a lump in Diamondbacks pitcher Doug Davis's throat. It concerned them enough to order tests and further examination. And then, with just six days remaining before the regular season started, they delivered the diagnosis: thyroid cancer. But along with that bad news, they offered Davis a positive outlook. Thyroid cancer affects approximately 18,000 people in the United States each year, but it is highly curable; his doctors thought that Davis would be able to return to the mound within six weeks of surgery.

Davis underwent surgery on April 10. Twenty-six days later, he threw 65 pitches in a simulated game, and on May 23, just 44 days after surgery, he started for the Diamondbacks in a game against the Braves. Davis won the game after pitching seven strong innings and allowing just one run on five hits. His teammates greeted him with a group hug when he left the game, but he admitted afterward that it wasn't as easy as he made it look. "It was kind of hard to control the emotions sometimes," he said, "because I'm excited to be back, and I'm anxious to throw my pitches."

A 6-foot-5 hurler, Dan Haren notched a combined
429 strikeouts in 2008 and 2009 and represented
Arizona in the All-Star Game both years.

DAN HAREN

Catcher Miguel Montero was a rapidly improving hitter in Arizona's lineup during the 2009 season, bopping 16 homers and batting close to .300.

MIGUEL MONTERO

Arizona fans hoped that third baseman Mark Reynolds and outfielder
Chris Young (right) would help propel the club back among the ranks
of the NL contenders in 2011 and beyond.

Arizona sputtered again in 2010, going 65–97, with a roster featuring such

young players as right fielder Justin Upton, Venezuelan-born catcher

Miguel Montero, and reliable hitter and shortstop Stephen Drew, the

Diamondbacks looked toward a brighter future.

Throughout their short history in the big leagues, the Diamondbacks

have had several exceptionally hot seasons—which is exactly what

fans in the desert city of Phoenix were hoping for when the team was

established. But Arizona fans have been willing to stick with their young

team during the cold spells as well. They know that their Diamondbacks

will snake their way back to the top soon.

INDEX